RELEASED FROM CIRCULATION

JAN 0 5 2020

EWALD BRANCH
GROSSE POINTE PUBLIC LIBRARY
GROSSE POINTE, MI 48236

FRILLED-NECK LIZARD

By Catherine C. Finan

Consultant: Darin Collins, DVM
Director, Animal Health Programs, Woodland Park Zoo

Minneapolis, Minnesota

Credits

cover, © Ken Griffiths/iStock; 3, © kkaplin/Shutterstock; 4, © Ken Griffiths/Shutterstock; 6, © Ken Griffiths/Shutterstock; 8, © Matt Cornish/Shutterstock; 9, © Bildagentur Zoonar GmbH/Shutterstock; 10, © Matt Cornish/Shutterstock; 11, © Ken Griffiths/iStock; 13, © I Wayan Sumatika/Shutterstock; 14, © Tomasz Klejdysz/Shutterstock; 14, © Thai siam/Shutterstock; 15, © I Wayan Sumatika/Shutterstock; 16, © Ken Griffiths/Shutterstock; 17, © Matt Cornish/Shutterstock; 18, © Auscape International Pty Ltd/Alamy Stock Photo; 20, © Tony Baggett/Shutterstock; 21, © DWI YULIANTO/Shutterstock; 23, © I Wayan Sumatika/Shutterstock

President: Jen Jenson
Director of Product Development: Spencer Brinker
Editor: Allison Juda
Designer: Micah Edel

Library of Congress Cataloging-in-Publication Data

Names: Finan, Catherine C., 1972- author.
Title: Frilled-neck lizard / Catherine C. Finan.
Description: Minneapolis, Minnesota : Bearport Publishing Company, [2021] |
  Series: Library of awesome animals | Includes bibliographical references and index.
Identifiers: LCCN 2020014009 (print) | LCCN 2020014010 (ebook) |
  ISBN 9781647471415 (library binding) | ISBN 9781647471521 (paperback) |
  ISBN 9781647471637 (ebook)
Subjects: LCSH: Frilled lizard—Juvenile literature.
Classification: LCC QL666.L223 F56 2021 (print) | LCC QL666.L223 (ebook)
  | DDC 597.95/5—dc23
LC record available at https://lccn.loc.gov/2020014009
LC ebook record available at https://lccn.loc.gov/2020014010

Copyright © 2021 Bearport Publishing Company. All rights reserved. No part of this publication may be reproduced in whole or in part, stored in any retrieval system, or transmitted in any form or by any means, electronic, mechanical, photocopying, recording, or otherwise, without written permission from the publisher.

For more information, write to Bearport Publishing, 5357 Penn Avenue South, Minneapolis, MN 55419. Printed in the United States of America.

Contents

Awesome Frilled-Neck Lizards! 4
What's in a Name? 6
Modern-Day Dragon 8
At Home in the Trees 10
Tiny Egg to Little Lizard 12
Time to Eat! 14
The Frill Is Up! 16
The Great Escape 18
A Famous Lizard 20

Information Station 22
Glossary 23
Index 24
Read More 24
Learn More Online 24
About the Author.................... 24

AWESOME

Frilled-Neck Lizards!

WHOOSH! A frilled-neck lizard's neck skin opens like an umbrella. It hisses a warning. From its fancy frill to the tip of its tail, the frilled-neck lizard is awesome!

THIS LIZARD'S FRILL CAN BE 12 INCHES (30 CM) ACROSS!

What's in a Name?

Take one look at a frilled-neck lizard and you'll see how it got its name! It has a colorful flap, or frill, of skin around its head. It uses the frill to appear larger—and scarier—when it needs to.

The frilled-neck lizard is also called the frilled lizard, the frillneck, and the coolest name of all . . . the frilled dragon!

SOME SCIENTISTS THINK THE LIZARD'S FRILL MAY HELP IT WARM UP WHEN IT LIES IN THE SUN.

Modern-Day Dragon

Dragons aren't real. But frilled-neck lizards come pretty close! They are part of the dragon family of lizards. Don't worry, though—they aren't monsters! Even though these lizards look a bit like dragons, they're much smaller (and they don't breathe fire)! Lizards in the dragon family all have wide heads and five toes on each foot.

A FRILLNECK CAN GROW ABOUT 3 FEET (0.9 M) LONG FROM HEAD TO TAIL. IT WEIGHS ONLY ABOUT 1 POUND (0.5 KG).

At Home in the Trees

The frilled-neck lizard makes its home in the dry forests of Australia. It spends most of its life up in the trees.

Male lizards come to the ground to fight over **territory** and females to **mate** with. The males raise their frills and push each other around. The winner gets the territory—and the female!

Tiny Egg to Little Lizard

Male and female lizards usually mate between October and November. Then, the female lays one or two **clutches** of eggs in an **underground** nest. There can be 6 to 20 eggs in a clutch.

After about 70 days, the frilled-neck lizard babies **hatch**. The little lizards can hunt and use their neck frills right away.

> FRILLED-NECK LIZARDS CAN LIVE FOR UP TO 20 YEARS.

A young frilled-neck lizard

Time to Eat!

Frilled-neck lizards sometimes come down to the ground to get some grub! Insects are a common snack. They dine on beetles, ants, termites, moths, and butterflies. Sometimes they'll feast on smaller lizards or mice.

Frilled-neck lizards stay very still until their dinner walks by. Then, they pounce on their **prey**. SURPRISE!

FRILLED-NECK LIZARDS HAVE EXCELLENT EYESIGHT. THIS HELPS THEM SPOT TASTY TREATS.

The Frill Is Up!

When they aren't grabbing a bite on the ground, frilled-neck lizards stay in the trees, where they hide from **predators**. The brown and gray colors on their scaly bodies help them blend in with tree bark.

But if a predator spots a frillneck, the show begins! The lizard opens its pink or yellow mouth wide. Then, it opens its brightly colored frill and hisses. **YIKES!**

FRILLED-NECK LIZARD PREDATORS INCLUDE SNAKES, DINGOES, AND BIRDS OF PREY.

The Great Escape

If the frilled-neck lizard's usual tricks don't work, it might **charge** at the predator. GO AWAY!

If *that* doesn't work, the lizard turns and runs away on its two back legs! It doesn't stop until it reaches a nearby tree. Then, it uses its sharp claws and long tail to climb to safety.

THE LIZARD'S STRANGE WAY OF RUNNING MAKES IT LOOK AS IF IT'S RIDING A BICYCLE. THAT'S WHY IT'S SOMETIMES CALLED THE BICYCLE LIZARD!

A Famous Lizard

When you think of Australian animals, the koala and kangaroo probably come to mind. But frilled-neck lizards are also well-loved animals in Australia. They've even appeared on Australian coins!

It's easy to see why these lizards are so famous. Just watch them put on their frilly shows and run around on two legs, and you'll agree—frilled-neck lizards are awesome!

An Australian coin

FRILLED-NECK LIZARDS ARE SOMETIMES KEPT AS PETS.

Information Station

FRILLED-NECK LIZARDS ARE AWESOME!
LET'S LEARN MORE ABOUT THEM.

Kind of animal: Frilled-neck lizards are reptiles. Reptiles are **cold-blooded** animals with scaly skin.

Other dragon lizards: There are over 300 kinds of dragon lizards! All dragon lizards are active during the day.

Size: Frilled-neck lizards can be up to 3 ft (0.9 m) from head to tail. That's the length of a guitar!

FRILLED-NECK LIZARDS AROUND THE WORLD

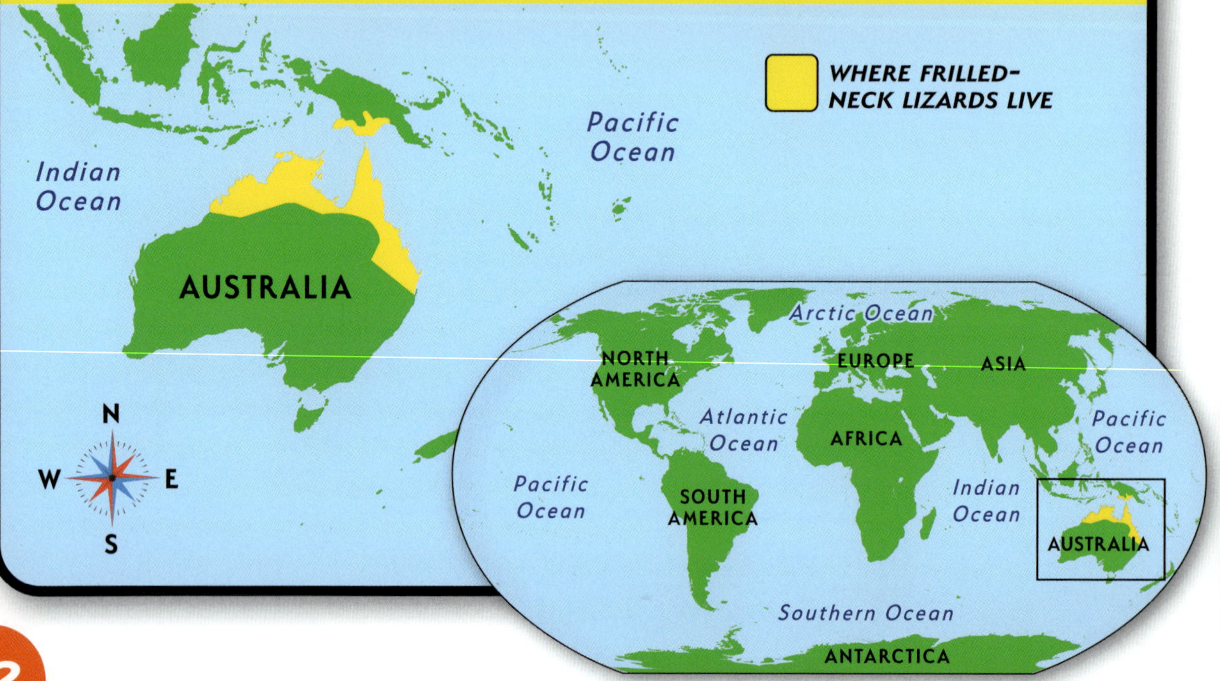

WHERE FRILLED-NECK LIZARDS LIVE

Indian Ocean

Pacific Ocean

AUSTRALIA

Arctic Ocean

NORTH AMERICA

EUROPE

ASIA

Atlantic Ocean

AFRICA

Pacific Ocean

Pacific Ocean

SOUTH AMERICA

Indian Ocean

AUSTRALIA

Southern Ocean

ANTARCTICA

Glossary

birds of prey birds such as hawks and eagles that feed on other animals

charge to rush toward

clutches nests of eggs

cold-blooded having blood that changes temperature depending on the temperature of the surrounding air or water

dingoes wild dogs found in Australia

hatch to come out of an egg

mate to come together to have young

predators animals that hunt and kill other animals for food

prey an animal that is hunted by another animal

territory an area that is marked and defended by a certain kind of animal

underground beneath Earth's surface

Index

Australia 10, 20
babies 12
dragon lizards 8, 22
frill 4, 6, 11–12, 16
hiss 4, 16
insects 14

mate 10, 12
predators 16, 18
prey 14
running 18
tail 4, 8, 18, 22
trees 10, 16, 18

Read More

Morey, Allan. *Frilled Lizards (Weird and Unusual Animals)*. Mankato, MN: Amicus Ink (2017).

Szymanski, Jennifer. *Real Dragons (National Geographic Reader)*. Washington, D.C.: National Geographic Kids (2018).

Wilsdon, Christina. *Ultimate Reptile-opedia: The Most Complete Reptile Reference Ever*. Washington, D.C.: National Geographic (2015).

Learn More Online

1. Go to **www.factsurfer.com**
2. Enter "**Frilled-Neck Lizard**" into the search box.
3. Click on the cover of this book to see a list of websites.

About the Author

Catherine C. Finan is a writer and nature lover living in northeastern Pennsylvania. One day she hopes to travel to Australia so she can see a frilled-neck lizard in person!